Meow!
Will you answer
the call for adventure?

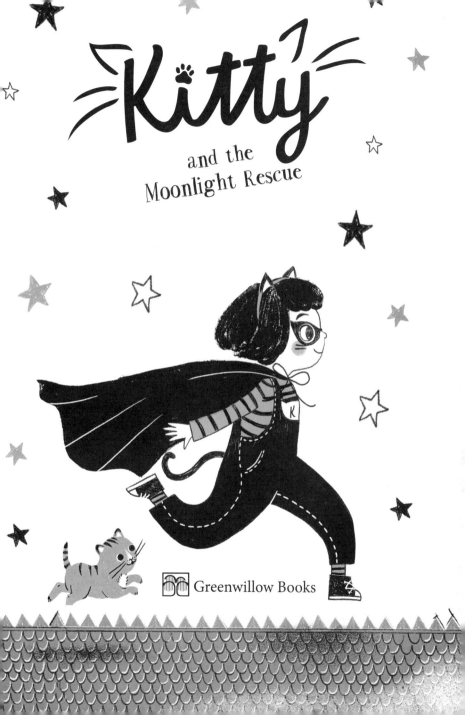

Kitty

and the
Moonlight Rescue

Greenwillow Books

For James, Abby, and Megan—P. H.

To my parents, who always let me roam free.
And to Murre, the best cat.—J. L.

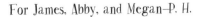

Kitty and the Moonlight Rescue
Text copyright © 2019 by Paula Harrison. Illustrations copyright © 2019 by Jenny Løvlie
First published in the United Kingdom in 2019 by Oxford University Press; first published in the United States by Greenwillow Books, 2019

www.harpercollinschildrens.com. The text of this book is set in Berling LT Std.

Library of Congress Cataloging-in-Publication Data

Names: Harrison, Paula, author. | Løvlie, Jenny, illustrator.
Title: Kitty and the moonlight rescue / written by Paula Harrison ; illustrated by Jenny Løvlie.
Description: First edition. | New York, NY : Greenwillow Books, an imprint of HarperCollins Publishers, 2019. | Series: Kitty ; 1 | Summary: Kitty wants to be a superhero like her mother, once she gets over her fear of the dark, but when Figaro the cat needs help she springs into action.
Identifiers: LCCN 2019016793| ISBN 9780062934710 (paperback) | ISBN 9780062934727 (hardcover)
Subjects: | CYAC: Superheroes—Fiction. | Human-animal Communication—Fiction. | Self-confidence—Fiction. | Fear of the dark—Fiction. | Cats—Fiction. | Adventure and adventurers—Fiction. | BISAC: JUVENILE FICTION / Readers / Chapter Books. | JUVENILE FICTION / Animals / Cats.
Classification: LCC PZ7.H256138 Kit 2019 | DDC [Fic]—dc23 LC record available at https://lccn.loc.gov/2019016793

20 21 22 23 PC/LSCC 10 9 8 7 6
First Edition

Greenwillow Books

Contents

Meet Kitty & Her Cat Crew

Kitty

Kitty has special powers—but is she ready to be a superhero just like her mom?

Luckily, Kitty's cat crew has faith in her and shows Kitty the hero that lies within.

Pumpkin

A stray ginger kitten who is utterly devoted to Kitty.

Figaro

Wise and kind, Figaro knows the neighborhood like the back of his paw.

Pixie

Pixie has a nose for trouble and whiskers for mischief!

Katsumi

Sleek and sophisticated, Katsumi is quick to call Kitty at the first sign of trouble.

Kitty

and the
Moonlight Rescue

Chapter 1

Kitty bounded into her mom and dad's bedroom as gracefully as a cat. She was wearing her stripy pajamas, and her dark hair bobbed around her face as she ran. Flipping head over heels, she landed neatly on the bed.

Her mom smiled. "Slow down, Kitty!

It's nearly bedtime. Aren't you sleepy yet?"

"No, I'm not tired at all!" Kitty watched her mom take a sleek black superhero outfit out of her wardrobe and put it on.

Kitty's family had a special secret. Her mom had catlike superpowers, and every night she went on adventures. Her mom could see in the dark, climb walls, and balance on rooftops. Her superpowered senses meant she could always tell when trouble was near. Best of all, she could talk to cats and share their secrets!

Kitty wanted to be a superhero just like her mom one day. She loved playing rescue in the cat outfit her dad had made her. She could leap all the way from the window seat to her bed without touching the floor.

But when she looked out the window at bedtime, there were so many mysterious shadows and odd noises out there. It was safe and snuggly in her room, and the thought of going out into the dark made her shiver. She wasn't sure if she would ever be ready to be a

superhero like her mom.

"Why don't you brush your teeth
and wash your face, Kitty?"
suggested Mom.

Her dad came in, carrying her little
brother. "It's time for you to brush
your teeth too, Max. Let's find
your toothbrush."

Kitty followed them to the bathroom, but Max giggled and scampered away at lightning speed.

Mom caught him and brought him back to the sink. "Be a good boy and do what your dad says, Max." She looked in the mirror and straightened her superhero mask. "It's getting late! I really must go."

"Can you read me a bedtime story first?" asked Kitty.

"I'm sorry, honey." Mom kissed Kitty on the forehead. "Maybe tomorrow night."

"I'll read you a story, Kitty," said Dad.

Kitty's shoulders slumped. She knew
being a superhero was important, but
she wished Mom didn't always rush off

at bedtime. "But I want *Mom* to tuck me in. I like our bedtime talks."

"Why don't we have a little talk now?" Mom took Kitty to her bedroom, and they sat on the window seat together.

It was growing dark outside, and a bright full moon was rising over the rooftops. An owl hooted in the distance.

"Having superpowers is a very special gift," said Mom, stroking Kitty's hair. "On a night like this, when the moon comes out, you can

feel magic in the air. Then you know it's the perfect time for an adventure."

Kitty stared at the darkening sky and shivered. The orange streetlamps were blinking on one by one, but strange shadows lingered at each corner. "It looks creepy out there. I don't think I could ever be a superhero and go out into the dark like you," Kitty said.

Mom hugged her tight. "You can choose to be whatever you want to be. But don't let fear hold you back. You're braver than you think!"

Kitty hugged her mom. "I will try to be brave! I just wish you didn't have to go."

"I know, but there are people out there who might need my help. Tomorrow we'll have pancakes for breakfast, and I'll tell you all about it." Mom smiled and gave her a kiss. "Sleep tight, darling. Remember, I won't be far away."

Kitty smiled back. "Night, Mom." She watched her mom climb out the window and run along the rooftops into the dark.

Dad read Kitty a bedtime story. Then she snuggled down and pulled the blanket up to her chin. Her bed was warm and comfortable, but she didn't feel ready to go to sleep yet. She wriggled onto her side and stared out the window.

The moon had risen high in the black sky, and shadows flickered on the rooftops. The wind whispered, and Kitty's heart beat faster. She turned on her bedside lamp and peeped over the

top of her blanket. *There's nothing to be scared of,* she told herself.

Her mom's words spun around inside her head: *"Don't let fear hold you back. You're braver than you think!"* Maybe she should put on her cat outfit and see if it made her feel any braver?

Jumping out of bed, she pulled her superhero costume over her head. Then she swung the silky black cape onto her shoulders and tied the ribbon carefully. Last of all, she put on her cat tail and velvety cat ears before turning to look in the mirror. She did a perfect spin, and the cape flew out behind her. She

loved the way the cat costume looked, and she did feel a tiny bit braver.

Suddenly there was a scratching

noise right outside her window. Kitty turned around, her eyes wide. The scratching grew louder, and then a shrill *meow* made her jump. She rushed to the window and peered into the dark.

A sleek black cat with a white stripe on his face and white paws was waiting on the window ledge. Kitty opened the window, and the cat sprang into the room with a flick of his tail.

"Good evening! My name

is Figaro." He smoothed his jet-black whiskers. "I must speak to your mother at once."

Kitty's heart skipped. Had she just understood what the cat said? "Hello, I'm Kitty," she managed.

"Lovely to meet you!" Figaro gave a theatrical bow. "Please take me to your mother, Kitty. There's an emergency, and I must get her help!"

Kitty's stomach did a somersault. "I'm sorry—my mom's already gone out. She left a little while ago."

Figaro clutched his cheek with one paw. "This is dreadful . . . but wait!" He stared at Kitty's cat costume. "You're a superhero too, so you can save us from this terrible disaster!"

"Oh, I can't really," said Kitty. "I wouldn't know what to do!"

"You *are* a superhero, though," insisted Figaro. "Who will help us if you don't?"

Kitty
looked nervously
at the night sky. She'd only
been pretending when she had
dressed up in the costume, but now
this cat believed she really *was*
a superhero. How could she
tell him that she didn't dare
go out into the dark?

Chapter 2

Kitty looked into the night. The thought of venturing outside made her feel wobbly inside, but how could she explain that to Figaro? He was expecting her to be a brave superhero. "What's happened?" she asked. "Is somebody hurt?"

Figaro leaped onto Kitty's bed and flicked his tail impatiently. "There's an awful noise coming from the clock tower, and the animals in the neighborhood

are in great distress! We have no idea what's making this dreadful racket. You must help!"'

Kitty leaned her head out the window. The clock tower was a long way from her house, but she could hear a terrible, high-pitched howling. It sent a shiver down her back.

"The clock tower is very tall, and the walls are too slippery for any of us to climb. There is panic out on the rooftops tonight, and we need your help."

Kitty's stomach lurched. The noise

could be anything! Did she really want to go and find out?

Figaro leaped neatly off the bed. He placed his paw on her knee, his face solemn. "Please, Kitty! We need you."

Kitty gulped. She wanted to help, and there was also a tiny part of her that wanted to see what it was like to have an adventure. She took a deep breath. "I'll go to the clock tower if you help me find the way."

Figaro's whiskers perked up. "Thank you, Kitty! Every cat in Hallam City will

be forever grateful." He skipped to the window, his white paws flashing. "Follow me, and I'll take you there at once."

Kitty's heart pounded as she climbed onto the windowsill. Clouds moved to hide the bright full moon, and the darkness thickened. For a second, Kitty nearly turned back inside. Then she took a deep breath and clambered through the window. She scrambled up from the windowsill and balanced on the roof, her heart racing.

The shadows seemed to stretch

toward her. She shivered as she gazed around, trying to spot the places she knew. There on the corner was Mr. Harvey's shop with all the cards and magazines in the window. Beyond that was the park, with its tall trees and duck pond. The clock tower looked very small in the distance.

The wind stirred and touched the back of Kitty's neck like a cold finger. A creature with wide wings swooped past with a terrible shriek. Kitty froze—her breath stuck in her throat.

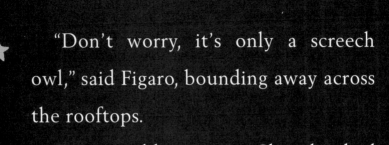

"Don't worry, it's only a screech owl," said Figaro, bounding away across the rooftops.

Kitty couldn't move. She clutched the chimney, and the bricks felt rough under her hands. She was just about to tell Figaro she wasn't really a superhero when suddenly there was a break in the clouds.

Moonlight poured over the rooftops, turning everything soft and silver. Kitty felt her magical superpowers tingling. She narrowed her eyes and turned on her nighttime vision. Then she listened carefully and found she could hear lots of tiny nighttime sounds, from insects chirping to the whispering of the wind in the trees.

Kitty let go of the chimney and felt her super balance kick in. It felt amazing! She skipped across the rooftops, light as a moonbeam.

"Come on—this way!" called Figaro, leaping from one roof to the next.

Kitty jumped across easily. Then she tried a somersault and landed on her toes. Figaro nodded approvingly. Kitty smiled at him.

The wind changed direction, and the terrible howling from the clock tower grew louder.

Figaro shook his head. "It's getting worse. We have to hurry!"

They ran along the next rooftop. Then Figaro stopped suddenly, scratching his ear. "This is no good! That's much too far to jump," he said.

Kitty crept onto a narrow ledge. "I think I can see a way across." She climbed up the gutter and ran past a row of chimneys. A strange shape moved on the opposite roof. Kitty swallowed. It looked like a monster with two heads. *It's just a shadow,* she told herself. *Remember . . . you're braver than you think!* When she looked again, she realized it was only the shadow of an oddly shaped tree.

She bent her knees and got ready to jump to the opposite roof.

"Help me!" called a little voice. "Somebody please help me!"

Kitty zoomed in on the sound with her super hearing. "Wait, Figaro!

Someone's in trouble. I think it's coming from the park." She clambered down the drainpipe and ran to the park entrance.

"Dear, dear!" Figaro puffed a little as he reached the ground. "What a terrible night we're having!"

Leaving the city streets behind, Kitty and Figaro raced along the winding path that led through the park. The darkness wrapped around them like a blanket, and there was a crackling in the bushes. Kitty swallowed. It was dark so far away from the streetlights and the houses.

The path forked. Kitty hesitated, listening again for the cry.

"I'll search this way." Figaro waved a paw before disappearing in the direction of the pond.

Kitty took the other path, her night vision sharpening. As she dashed around a bend, she caught a glimpse of orange fur. A fox with a white-tipped tail lurked at the bottom of a tree. It glanced at Kitty and raised its black nose to sniff the air. Kitty backed away. The fox had a sharp glint in its eyes.

"Help me!" called a tiny voice from the branches above.

Kitty's heart raced. Someone was trapped up there! She ran forward and the fox dashed away, its tail flashing in the moonlight.

Kitty peered up into the dark web of

leaves. "It's all right! I've come to help you."

There was no answer. Hairs prickled on the back of Kitty's neck.

"My name's Kitty. Are you okay?"

The silence thickened.

A fluttery feeling grew in Kitty's chest. Even superpowered sight wouldn't let her see through the tangle of leaves. Who was up there, and why wouldn't they speak to her?

Kitty gulped. There was only one way to learn who had been calling for

help. Finding a foothold in the trunk, she pulled herself onto the lowest tree branch and began to climb.

Chapter 3

Kitty swung from one branch to the next, and the leaves above her moved wildly. No matter how quickly she climbed, someone else was climbing away from her even faster.

"Wait! I came to help you," called Kitty.

The rustling stopped, and a pair of bright eyes blinked over the edge of a thick branch. "Are you sure you're not a monster?" said a little voice.

Kitty realized she was speaking to a cat. "I promise I'm not a monster. I'm just a girl who can talk to cats. It's a special talent that runs in my family," she explained. "I won't hurt you."

"Oh!" The eyes blinked again. "My name's Pixie." The leaves shook, and a small cat with fluffy white fur jumped onto Kitty's branch.

"What happened? Did the fox scare you?" asked Kitty.

"I was up here in the tree, imagining I was a magical cat with wings. Then that horrible howling started. Can you hear it? I think it's a g-g-ghost!" Pixie's whiskers trembled.

"Figaro says it's coming from the clock tower. I'm on my way to investigate right now," said Kitty.

Pixie clutched Kitty's arm with her paw. "You mustn't! What if the ghost sees you?"

Kitty swallowed. "I'm sure it isn't a ghost," she said firmly. "Why don't you come with us and see for yourself? The fox is gone, so it's quite safe to climb down."

Pixie followed Kitty down the tree, still muttering about ghosts and monsters. Kitty was starting to wonder if the little cat had a very strong imagination. They scrambled through the bushes to find Figaro scampering toward them. At his side was a tabby cat with serious amber eyes.

"There you are, Kitty!" Figaro twirled his whiskers. "I was getting so worried! Pixie, what on earth are you doing here?"

"I was up a tree dreaming of becoming a cat with wings! But now Kitty says I should come and look for the clock tower ghost," replied Pixie.

Figaro tutted. "Dear me! I see you're full of wild ideas, as usual." He waved to the cat with the amber eyes. "Kitty, I'd like you to meet my friend Katsumi.

She's brought some news about the clock tower emergency."

"Pleased to meet you," the tabby cat said, bowing her head. She had a beautiful honey-colored coat and a long, elegant tail.

"Hello, Katsumi!" Pixie bounced up to the tabby cat, and they touched noses.

"Katsumi, this is my new friend Kitty," said Figaro. "She has special superpowers just like her mother, so I asked her to help us."

Kitty's stomach lurched. "I'm not

really a superhero—"

"Of course you are!" Figaro interrupted, turning to Katsumi. "Well, what is the news from the clock tower?"

"An owl friend told me there's a creature on the tower," explained Katsumi. "He didn't get close enough to see what it was, but he seemed quite shaken. The noise was overwhelming!"

Kitty listened. She didn't need super senses to detect the sound coming from the clock tower anymore. The wailing noise was growing louder and sharper.

"I know a shortcut," said
Katsumi. "Follow me."

Kitty and the others followed
Katsumi across the park. It was strange
seeing the place at night. Moonlight

glinted on the swings and the slide, and the duck pond shined like a silver coin.

Leaves crackled, and a little owl with white and brown feathers flew down to perch on the branch of a tree. Katsumi nodded to the bird. The owl hooted before spreading its wings and flying away into the dark.

Leaving the park, they passed a row of shops. Figaro stopped outside a seafood store and licked his lips. "Goodness me! That haddock looks delicious." His stomach gave a deep rumble.

Just then, the crying from the clock tower rose into a sharp wail. The noise was so sad and lonely that it made Kitty's heart ache. "Quickly!" she called to the cats. "We're nearly there." She raced down a little alley that took her

into a small square surrounded by houses.

The clock tower was right in front of her, pointing into the clouds. The huge clockface was as round and pale as the full moon hanging in the sky. The hands on the clock pointed to five minutes to midnight.

Kitty's night vision grew stronger as she stared at the tower's smooth stone walls. She focused on the terrible noise and spotted a tiny ball huddled on a narrow ledge. It wasn't a ghost or a terrifying monster. It was a little ginger kitten. Its tail was curled around its body and its blue eyes were wide with fright.

"There's a kitten on a ledge close

to the top of the tower," Kitty told the others. "I don't know how he got so high."

"Goodness me!" said Figaro. "How can one little kitten make such a terrible racket?"

"It doesn't even sound like a kitten," said Pixie, swishing her tail.

"There's a way onto the roof over there." Katsumi pointed to a house with a low porch. "Go on, Kitty, there's no time to lose."

Kitty nodded, grateful for Katsumi's

sensible ideas. She climbed onto the porch and from there to the rooftop. The others followed her. The kitten looked down, shivering wildly.

The huge clockface below the kitten showed the time: four minutes to twelve o'clock.

Kitty took a sharp breath. Soon it would be midnight, and the clock would make twelve deafening chimes. The noise was bound to startle the kitten. What if it surprised him so much that he fell right off the ledge? "Don't be frightened!" she called to the little cat "I'm Kitty, and this is Figaro, Pixie, and Katsumi. We've come to help you."

The kitten stared down at them. "YOOOWL!" he cried, and tears dripped down his furry cheeks.

"Poor thing!" said Katsumi. "I wonder how he got stuck."

"He's very young to climb all the way to that ledge." Figaro shook his head. "Kittens these days can be so reckless!"

Pixie turned her eyes to Kitty. "You will help him, won't you?"

Kitty's stomach felt wobbly. "I want to try!" she stammered. "But I'm not really a superhero. I've never been on an adventure before."

"But you were wearing your superhero outfit!" exclaimed Figaro.

"It's just for playing!" said Kitty desperately. "I'm not sure I can do this."

"You've already come this far," said Katsumi. "And superpowers clearly run in your family."

Figaro frowned. "Yes! Just remember how courageously you dashed into the pitch-black park when you heard Pixie's cry for help. I thought to myself at the time how brave you were!"

Pixie nodded eagerly. "I could have been up that tree all night if it wasn't for you."

Kitty blushed at their kind words. She thought again of what her mom had said: *"You're braver than you think."* She turned to face the huge tower, and her head spun at the thought of climbing up so high. Then she looked at the tiny ginger kitten, scrabbling at the side of the ledge.

Kitty closed her eyes and felt her powers tingling inside her. "That kitten's in terrible danger. I know I have to do something!"

A steep drop stretched below her

with a narrow stone ledge on the other side. Deep shadows filled the chasm, and the cold wind ruffled Kitty's hair. She took a big breath. Then she sprang across, landing neatly on the other side. Gripping the stone wall with her fingertips, she began to climb.

Chapter 4

Kitty climbed the clock tower swiftly, digging her fingers into the gaps between the smooth stones.

"You can do it!" Pixie cried.

The steep drop below was filled with darkness, but moonlight poured over the tower, turning the stones silver. Kitty felt her superpowers rushing through her, and her heart skipped. Maybe she could be a superhero like her mom after all!

Pulling herself onto the next ledge, she stopped for a second to catch her breath. The ginger kitten peered down at her with wide eyes. There was a sudden click as the big hand on the clock moved closer to the twelve, and the kitten jumped with fright. Kitty's chest tightened. It was such a long way down.

She climbed faster, her arms and legs tingling. She could hear the ticking of the clock. With a loud click, the big hand shifted to point straight at the number twelve. It was midnight!

"Don't be scared!" called Kitty. "The clock is about to chime."

The kitten shook as he gripped the ledge. "What's a chime?"

Bong! The clock made a deep sound. It was so loud that the whole tower trembled. Kitty held on tightly.

The tiny ginger cat jumped in fright,

then toppled backward, tumbling down the clockface with a terrified mew.

"No!" Kitty shouted.

The kitten clutched at the clock's long hand and clung to it desperately.

The hand slid back to point at the number eleven. The kitten hung there. He wailed while his legs swung wildly in midair.

"Don't let go! I'll come to get you." Kitty's powers tingled, and she climbed faster. She had to reach the kitten in time!

Kitty scrambled down . . . ten, eleven, twelve. Just as the last chime rang out, a strong gust of wind swirled around the tower. The ginger kitten swayed wildly, and he lost his grip with one paw.

Kitty's heart pounded. She couldn't let him fall!

"We believe in you, Kitty!" Figaro shouted from below.

"Go on, Kitty!" Katsumi called out. "You can do it."

Pixie jumped up and down, one paw over her mouth.

Kitty stepped onto the ledge below the clockface. The ginger kitten was still dangling from the clock hand, and there was no easy way to reach him. Kitty took a deep breath and climbed

onto the closest number, her black cape billowing out in the wind.

Using her superpowers to balance, she clambered from one number to the next and steadied herself. She was just below the kitten. His back paws dangled above her head.

"I'm here to rescue you!" she told him. "Reach down and take my hand."

The kitten's legs swung. "I can't—I'm stuck!"

"You've been so brave," said Kitty. "I promise I won't let you fall."

The kitten gazed at Kitty with terrified blue eyes. "I can't move!"

"Be brave!" urged Kitty. "I know you can do it."

The kitten's whiskers quivered and he reached down, letting Kitty grab hold of his paw. He let go of the clock hand, and Kitty caught him and pulled him close. She could feel his body shaking. The wind swirled around them, and Kitty held tight to the clockface. There was still a long way to go before they reached safety.

"Hold on to my shoulders," Kitty told the little cat. "Then I'll have my hands free to climb."

The kitten scrambled onto her shoulders. Kitty made her way down the tower, careful to keep her balance. The kitten clung to her neck as he peered anxiously at the ground.

"It's too far!" he squeaked. "We'll never make it."

"We will," Kitty told him. "Can you see my friends on that rooftop over there? Soon you'll be able to meet them."

The kitten looked at the rooftop, his whiskers twitching. Kitty kept climbing, but the kitten clutched at her face, covering her eyes with his paws.

Kitty didn't want to worry him, so instead she used her superpowered senses. She felt along the tower wall for every foothold and handhold, balancing perfectly. She could hear Figaro and Katsumi talking, so she knew exactly where she was going. At last they reached the wide ledge where she had begun her climb.

"Are you ready?" Kitty asked the ginger cat. "I'm going to jump across."

"You mean—all the way over there?" he squeaked, staring at the gap between the clock tower and the rooftop. "It's too far, we'll both fall!"

"Don't worry, I've done this before."

Kitty smiled. "And I have superpowers that help me."

The kitten's eyes grew big and round. "Then you're a real superhero?"

"I'm still learning," said Kitty. "And this is my very first adventure!"

The little cat gazed at her solemnly. "I trust you! I will hold tight while you jump."

Kitty got ready, bending her knees and throwing back her arms. Then she made an enormous leap. Her black cape swirled out behind her, and for a moment, Kitty felt as though she was flying through the sky. She landed softly on the other side and set the kitten down on the rooftop. Figaro,

Katsumi, and Pixie rushed over to meet them, mewing with excitement.

"That was such a daring rescue!" gasped Pixie. "Were you scared, Kitty?"

"A little bit," Kitty admitted. "But I knew all of you believed in me, and that helped a lot."

"You certainly have great climbing skills," said Katsumi. "Don't you agree, Figaro?"

"Yes, indeed!" Figaro twirled his whiskers. "But I do think it was very silly of this kitten to be up so high in the first place." He turned to the kitten. "What in paw's name were you doing up there?"

The little cat's nose twitched, and

a tear rolled down his furry cheek. "I was searching for somewhere warm to sleep. I thought if I climbed up high it would be easier to look. Then I realized

I was too high and I couldn't get down."

Kitty crouched beside him. "Please don't cry! What's your name? Do you have any family or friends nearby who can look after you?"

The kitten shook his head. "I don't have any family or friends. I don't have a name, either."

Kitty was surprised. How could this lovely kitten not even have a name? "We'd love to be your friends if you'd like that." She looked at the other cats, and they nodded in agreement.

The kitten wiped a tear away with his paw, and a smile spread across his face. "I'd like that more than anything in the world!"

Chapter 5

Kitty sat down on the rooftop next to the kitten. The streets below were dark and silent. Stars glittered overhead like diamonds scattered across the sky.

"Where do you usually like to sleep?" she asked him.

"I like to find somewhere warm and bright. The thing is . . ." The kitten twitched his ears shyly. "I'm a little bit scared of the dark."

"Sometimes I feel like that too, especially when the clouds cover up the moon and there are lots of shadows." Kitty looked from her friends to the beautiful night sky. She smiled, remembering what her mom had told her. "But the nighttime isn't as frightening as I thought. When the moon comes out, you can feel magic in the air."

The kitten nodded.

His eyes were wide.

"Where will you go now?" Figaro asked the kitten. "I'm afraid my humans won't let me bring visitors into our home. I tried it once, and it caused such a kerfuffle!" The kitten's shoulders drooped. "I don't know. Sometimes I sleep outside the seafood store and the shopkeeper gives me some fish when the shop opens in the morning, but the doorstep is cold and hard."

"You must come with me!" said Kitty firmly. "Everyone in my family loves cats. You can sleep in my room, and I'll make you a delicious breakfast in the morning."

The kitten perked up. "Really? I can come with you?"

Kitty smiled. "Of course you can! And tomorrow you can meet my family."

The kitten bounced up and down with happiness. "I've always wanted to see inside a real home. Thank you, Kitty!"

Kitty led the cats down from the roof and back through the square. When they reached the park, the kitten began to tremble. He yowled at a spiky bush and jumped into Kitty's arms.

"What's wrong?" asked Kitty.

"It looks like a monster!" squeaked the kitten.

"Don't worry—it's nothing to be scared of." Kitty set him down, but a moment later he hopped back into her arms when a tree branch rustled in the wind.

Kitty carried him through the park and he yowled at the gate, the pond, and the swings. At last his head began to droop. He gave one final squeaky mew at a park bench before closing his eyes. His head rested on Kitty's shoulder.

"Poor thing!" whispered Pixie. "It must be awful finding everything so scary."

Figaro rolled his eyes. "Things are certainly quieter now that he's asleep. For goodness sake, don't wake him up again!"

Kitty and her friends hurried out

of the park and climbed back to the rooftops. They darted along, skipping neatly around the chimneys. At last Kitty spotted her bedroom window at the end of a row of houses. She had left her lamp on, and it glowed behind the curtains.

"Thank you for helping me with my very first adventure," she said to Figaro, Katsumi, and Pixie.

"It was our pleasure," said Katsumi with a bow.

"You did a fantastic job! I expect now

you'll want to go on more," said Figaro
with a wink.

"I expect I will!" said Kitty, laughing.

The ginger kitten woke up and waved
his paw sleepily. "Goodbye, everyone,
and thank you!"

"Goodbye! See you again soon," said
Kitty.

Kitty watched Figaro, with his handsome black coat and white paws, scamper away across the rooftops. Katsumi followed him, her honey-colored fur pale in the moonlight. Pixie left last, her bright white fur gleaming in the darkness.

Kitty sighed happily. It really had

been an amazing night!

She set the kitten down on the windowsill and climbed into her bedroom. "I hope you like my room. I have lots of comfy pillows and blankets. Would you like to come and see?"

The kitten's whiskers shook. "I . . . I don't really know! I thought I wanted to see a real home, but . . . what if I get trapped inside?"

"You won't! And I promise I'll look after you," said Kitty, surprised.

The kitten backed away to the corner

of the windowsill. "I can't go
in! Please don't be mad!"

"Don't worry, I'm not mad!"
Kitty reached out and stroked

the kitten between his ears. "I just don't want you to be cold."

"I'm quite warm here." The kitten lay down on the windowsill and curled his tail around his body.

Kitty fetched her pillows and a blanket and brought them over to the window seat. She left the window open and settled down on the wide, cushioned seat so that she could be close to the ginger kitten. She could see his striped tummy rising and falling peacefully as he slept.

Kitty hoped he was having happy dreams. At last she closed her eyes too, and the stars twinkled above them in the velvet-black sky.

Chapter 6

When Kitty woke up the next morning, her mom was pushing the hair out of her face. She sat bolt upright, puzzled to find herself on the window seat and not in bed. Then she remembered everything that had happened the night before. She peeked through the open window, but the kitten wasn't asleep on the sill anymore.

"Morning, Kitty!" said Mom. "You look like you had an adventure last night."

Kitty glanced down at her superhero

outfit. "It was amazing! A cat named Figaro came here looking for you. It was an emergency, so I went to help instead."

"Shall I make us some breakfast? And then you can tell me all about it," said Mom.

"Ooh, yes please! But..." Kitty peered outside, frowning. "Can you see a little ginger kitten? When I went to sleep, he was right here on the windowsill."

Throwing off her blanket, she leaned out the window and listened carefully.

All she could hear were birds chirping
and cars driving along the street below.
Kitty's heart sank. She'd wanted to
look after the kitten because he had no
home of his own. She wished he'd been
brave enough to come inside.

"Maybe he's still nearby," said Mom.
"Why don't you try going outside and
calling him?"

Kitty slipped out the window and
climbed to the rooftop. The sun shined
down warmly, and wisps of clouds hung
in the pale blue sky. Kitty stopped on

the ridge of the roof, calling, "Hello, are you still here?"

At first there was no answer. Then a small striped face with whiskers peeped out from behind the chimney. His blue eyes lit up when he saw Kitty. Then he drew back nervously.

Mom, who had followed Kitty, whispered, "Is he a shy cat?"

"I think he's nervous because he's been living all alone until now," explained Kitty. "He didn't want to come inside last night. He's not used to having a home."

"I see." Mom frowned thoughtfully. "Well, if he won't come to us, maybe we should go to him. Come and help me with the breakfast things, Kitty."

Kitty and her mom made a stack of golden pancakes that smelled so delicious they made Kitty's mouth water. They carried the pancakes out

to the rooftop, along with some fresh
orange juice. They also brought out
some fresh fish in case the kitten was
hungry. They spread Kitty's blanket on

a small, flat area of the roof near the chimney.

Kitty poured some syrup on her pancake and took a bite. "Mmm! Everything tastes better when you eat outside."

"It really does!" said her mom, laughing.

"I wonder if this fish tastes good too," said Kitty, glancing at the chimney.

The kitten's face peered out again, and his nose twitched as he smelled the breakfast. He crept up to the bowl of fish.

"Good morning!" Kitty beamed. "I hope you're hungry."

"Good morning." The kitten flicked his tail shyly and then nibbled some food from the bowl. "This fish is so yummy!"

"Did someone say fish?" Figaro

leaped along the rooftops, stopping to preen his sleek black-and-white fur. "I hope there's enough for me!"

Katsumi, who was behind him, waved her elegant tail. "Honestly, Figaro! You shouldn't invite yourself to someone else's meal."

Pixie, arriving last, sniffed the air. The sun gleamed on her silky white coat. "It does smell delicious. I can imagine I've walked into a splendid banquet!"

Katsumi bowed to Kitty and her mom. "Sorry for interrupting your breakfast!

We just came to say good morning and to thank Kitty for her help last night."

"Good morning!" Mom smiled. "You're welcome to join us. I have plenty more fish in the fridge."

"That is most kind!" exclaimed Figaro

while Katsumi and Pixie murmured their thanks.

Mom climbed inside and reappeared with three more bowls of food.

The ginger kitten finished his breakfast and licked the bowl with his little pink tongue. "That was delicious!" He crept over to Kitty and curled up in her lap.

Kitty smiled and stroked his fur gently.

"Good morning!" Dad lifted Max onto the rooftop. "Do I smell pancakes?"

Soon everyone was eating breakfast and talking about Kitty's adventure the night before. Figaro reminded them all that it had been his idea to fetch Kitty in the first place.

"I was certain Kitty's catlike superpowers would be just what we needed," he told everyone.

Kitty blushed. "I didn't think I could do it . . . but it got easier the more I tried!"

"I'm very proud of you, Kitty." Mom beamed at her before turning to the kitten. "And maybe you'd like to come live with us? We have plenty of room here, and we'd love you to stay. I'm sure it would be nicer than sleeping outside on some doorstep."

Kitty's heart skipped. She'd hoped her family would love the kitten as much as she did. She held her breath, waiting for him to reply.

"You *really* want me to stay?" He looked from Mom to Kitty. "Not just for one day, but forever?"

"Yes, please do!" Kitty stroked him

between the ears. "And I think we should help you to choose a name." She wrinkled her forehead, thinking. "How about Pumpkin? It suits you because you have such lovely orange fur."

The kitten purred. "I love that name!

Do you really think it suits me?"

"It's perfect for you!" Katsumi told him.

Pumpkin rubbed his face against Kitty's and she held him tight, feeling his soft fur against her cheek.

"I think . . . maybe one day soon . . . I'd like to go on another adventure in the moonlight," said Pumpkin.

"Are you sure you wouldn't be too scared of the dark?" asked Kitty.

Pumpkin thought hard about this. "Maybe a little bit, but it's much easier to be brave when I'm with you."

Kitty hugged him tight. She was so happy to have found Pumpkin, and she was looking forward to having another adventure, too!

Super Facts About Cats

Super Speed

Have you ever seen a cat make a quick escape from a dog? If so, you know they can move *really* fast—up to thirty miles per hour!

Super Hearing

Cats have an incredible sense of hearing and can swivel their ears to pinpoint even the tiniest of sounds.

Super Reflexes

Have you ever heard the saying, "Cats always land on their feet"? People say this because cats have amazing reflexes. If a cat

114

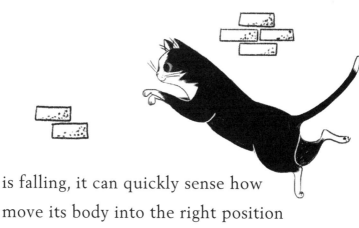

is falling, it can quickly sense how
to move its body into the right position
to land safely.

Super Vision

Cats have amazing nighttime vision. Their
incredible ability to see in low light allows
them to hunt for prey when it's dark outside.

Super Smell

Cats have a very powerful sense of smell.
Did you know that the pattern of ridges on
each cat's nose is as unique as a human's
fingerprints?

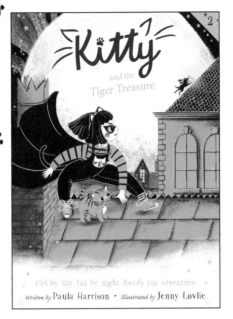

≋Kitty≋

and the
Tiger Treasure

Girl by day. Cat by night. Ready for adventure.

Written by Paula Harrison · *Illustrated by* Jenny Løvlie

What's next for Kitty?

Kitty can't wait to see the priceless Golden Tiger statue with her own eyes. Legend says that if you hold the statue, you can make your greatest wish come true. Kitty and her cat, Pumpkin, decide to sneak into the museum to see the statue at night, when no one else is around. But disaster strikes when the statue is stolen right in front of them! Can Kitty find the thief and return the precious statue before sunrise?

Here's a special sneak peek
of Book #2! Meow!

Kitty sprang from the sofa to the door in a single bound. "Stop right there!" She pointed her finger at Pumpkin the cat. "You won't get away with it this time!"

Pumpkin, a roly-poly ginger kitten with black whiskers, scampered out of reach. "Can't catch me!" he meowed, darting into Kitty's bedroom.

Kitty chased after him, giggling. Pumpkin leapt onto the bed and rolled over to let Kitty tickle his fluffy tummy.

Meet Kitty!

Girl by day.

Cat by night. Ready for adventure!

The Kitty books—read them all!

Is Kitty brave enough to step out into the darkness for a thrilling moonlight adventure?

Can Kitty find the thief who stole the tiger treasure and return the precious statue before sunrise?

Will Kitty save the wondrous and secret sky garden before it is destroyed forever?

Heroic teamwork and a magical feast bring Kitty and a new friend together!

Meowing Soon!

Kitty and the
Great Lantern Race

Kitty and the
Twilight Trouble